Mortimer Plays I-Spy

Gareth Stevens Publishing
A WORLD ALMANAC EDUCATION GROUP COMPANY

Mortimer's Fun with Words

For a free color catalog describing Gareth Stevens' list of high-quality books and multimedia programs, call 1-800-542-2595 (USA) or 1-800-461-9120 (Canada). Gareth Stevens Publishing's Fax: (414) 332-3567.

Library of Congress Cataloging-in-Publication Data available upon request from publisher.
Fax: (414) 332-3567 for the attention of the Publishing Records Department.

ISBN 0-8368-2749-X

This North American edition first published in 2000 by
Gareth Stevens Publishing
A World Almanac Education Group Company
330 West Olive Street, Suite 100
Milwaukee, WI 53212 USA

This edition © 2000 by Gareth Stevens, Inc. Original © BryantMole Books, 1999. First published in 1999
by Evans Brothers Limited, 2A Portman Mansions, Chiltern Street, London W1M 1LE, United Kingdom.
Additional end matter © 2000 by Gareth Stevens, Inc.

Created by Karen Bryant-Mole
Photographs by Zul Mukhida
Designed by Jean Wheeler
Teddy bear by Merrythought Ltd.

Printed in the United States of America

1 2 3 4 5 6 7 8 9 04 03 02 01 00

contents

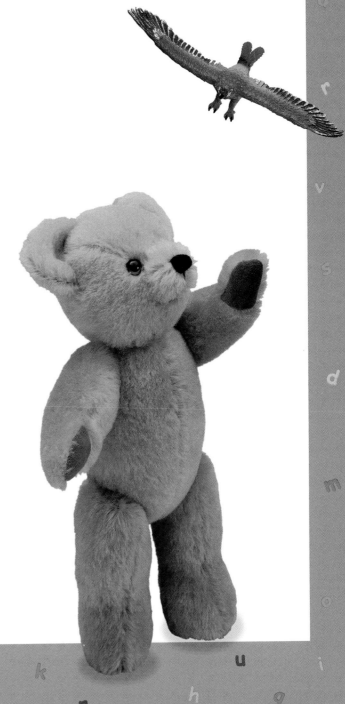

toys

Mortimer wants to play I-spy with you!

I spy something that begins with the letter **p**.

Can you find something that begins
with each of these letters?

d   b   k

food

Can you find something that begins with each of these letters?

c l p

wild animals

I spy something
that begins with
the letter **z**.

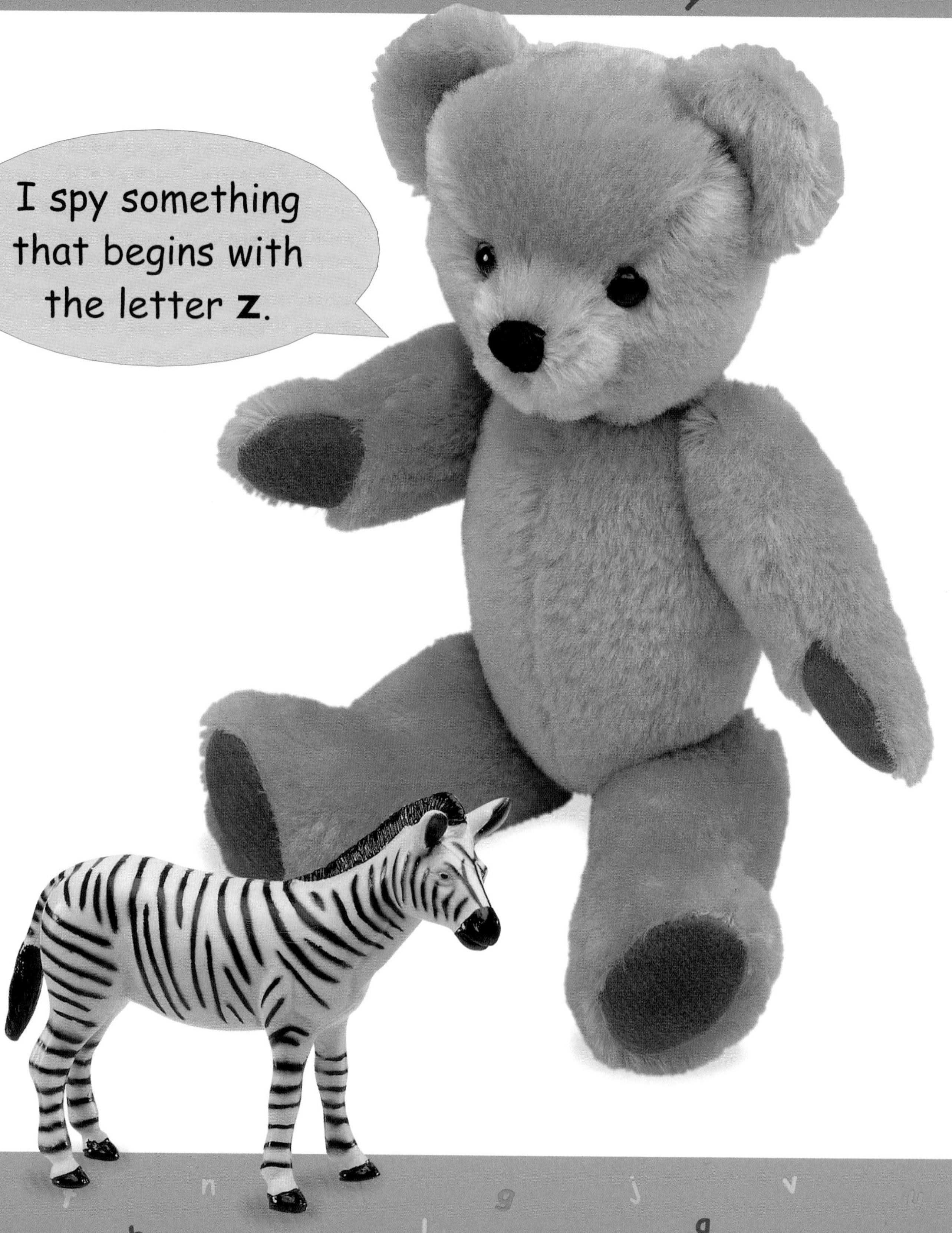

Can you find something that begins with each of these letters?

e   l

Can you find an animal that ends with the letter **x**?

weather

Can you find something
that begins with each
of these letters?

h   u   b

animal groups

I spy a group of animals that begins with the letter **b**.

Can you find the groups of animals that begin with each of these letters?

f **i**

kitchen tools

Can you find something
that begins with each
of these letters?

k w t

colors

I spy a color that begins with the letter **r**.

Can you find colors that begin
with each of these letters?

g   y   o

things that go

I spy something that begins with the letter **v**.

Can you find something that begins with each of these letters?

j h m

animal noises

I spy a duck. The noise it makes begins with the letter **q**.

What are the noises these animals make?
The noises begin with each of these letters.

m   **n**   **b**

alphabet

Can you name all the letters in the alphabet?

You can use these letters to play your own I-spy game!

a b c d e f
g h i j k
l m n o p
q r s t u
v w x y z

glossary/index

helicopter — a type of aircraft that uses propellers to stay in the air 19

kettle — a type of pot that is used to heat water or other liquids 15

motorcycle — a vehicle with two wheels and an engine that you ride on like a bike 19

rolling pin — a long, rounded object, often made of wood, that is used to flatten and roll out dough 14

spy — to see or watch something or someone, sometimes in a secret way 4, 6, 8, 10, 12, 14, 16, 18, 20, 23

van — a big, box-shaped vehicle with a closed back end that can be used to carry things and people 18

weather — the conditions outdoors that can be hot or cold, sunny or cloudy, windy or calm, rainy or dry 10

whisk — a kitchen tool that can be used to stir eggs or other foods 15

videos

Alphabet Soup. (Warner Studios)

The Animal Alphabet. (Warner Studios)

Blue's Clues: ABCs and 123s. (Paramount Studios)